SEARCHING

Olga de Dios

This is the story of a character
who was nicknamed Serch
because it was always searching.

THIS STORY IS DEDICATED
TO ALL PEOPLE
WHO REMAIN BY YOUR SIDE
WHEN YOU LOOK UP.

Searching
Somos8 Series

© Text and images: Olga de Dios, 2014
© Edition: NubeOcho, 2014
www.nubeocho.com – info@nubeocho.com

Original title: *Buscar*
English translation: Robin Sinclair
Typography: BOOKEND Joanne Abellar
The illustrations for this book were done by digital media.

First edition: September 2014
ISBN: 978 84 942929 8 9
Printed in Spain – Gráficas Jalón

It always walked with its head down.

All it could see was the ground.

Early one morning,
White Rabbit crossed
its way saying:

HELLO, WHAT ARE YOU DOING?

Serch answered
without looking up:

A short time later,
Serch walked by Ramona the Bear.

Serch answered still looking
at the ground:

SEARCHING

At noon Rosita
crossed its path.

HELLO, WHAT ARE YOU DOING?

And again, Serch answered:

Afterwards,
Trish and Tresh appeared.

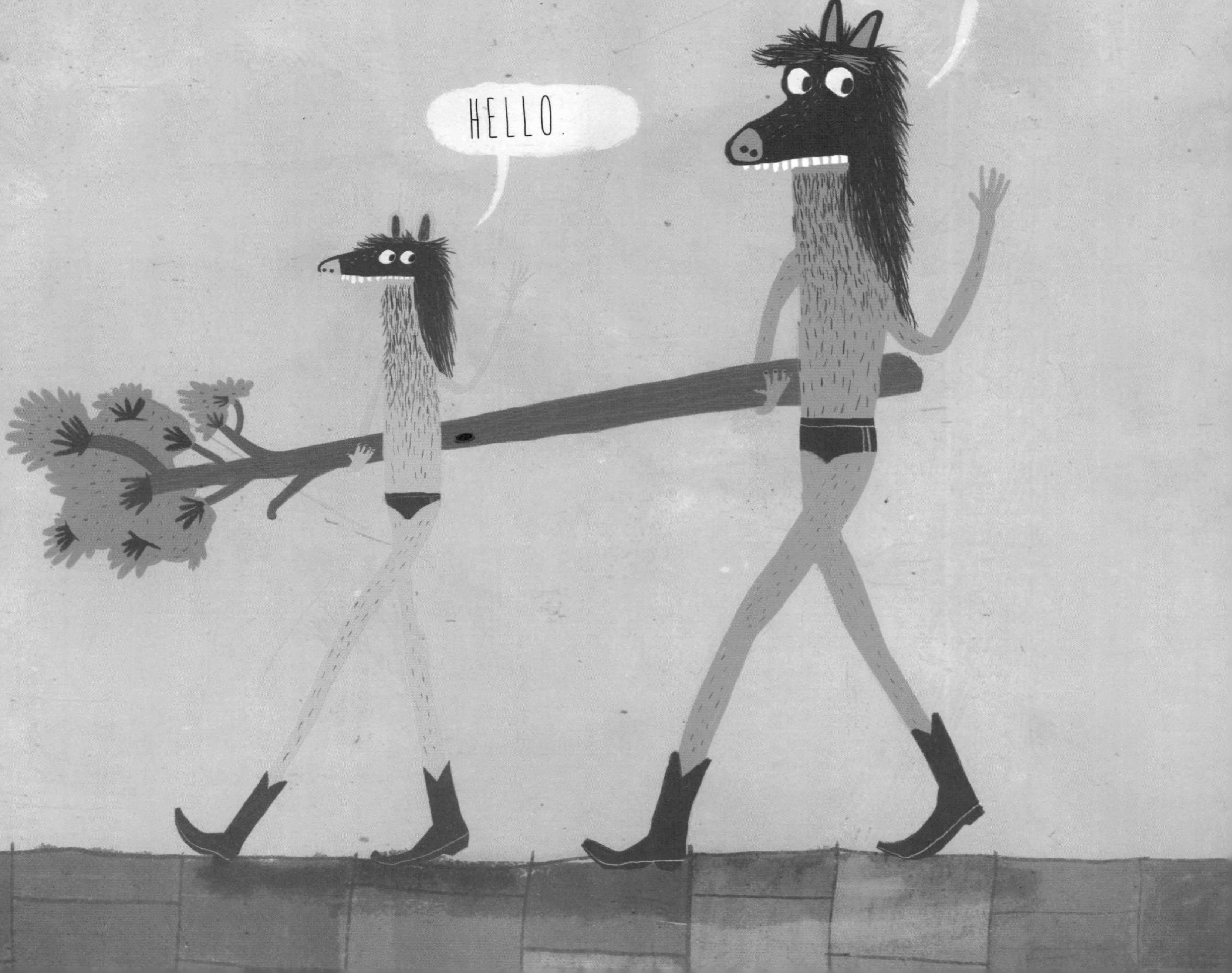

Once again Serch answered:

At lunchtime,
Orange and Lemon passed by
and shouted:

Serch answered while still looking at the ground:

In the afternoon, Serch
came across
Zeta, Aubergine, Agile
Turtle, Evarist the Artist,
Phoenix and Little Slug.

HELLO,
WHAT ARE
YOU DOING?

HELLO, WHAT ARE YOU DOING?

HELLO!

Serch always answered…

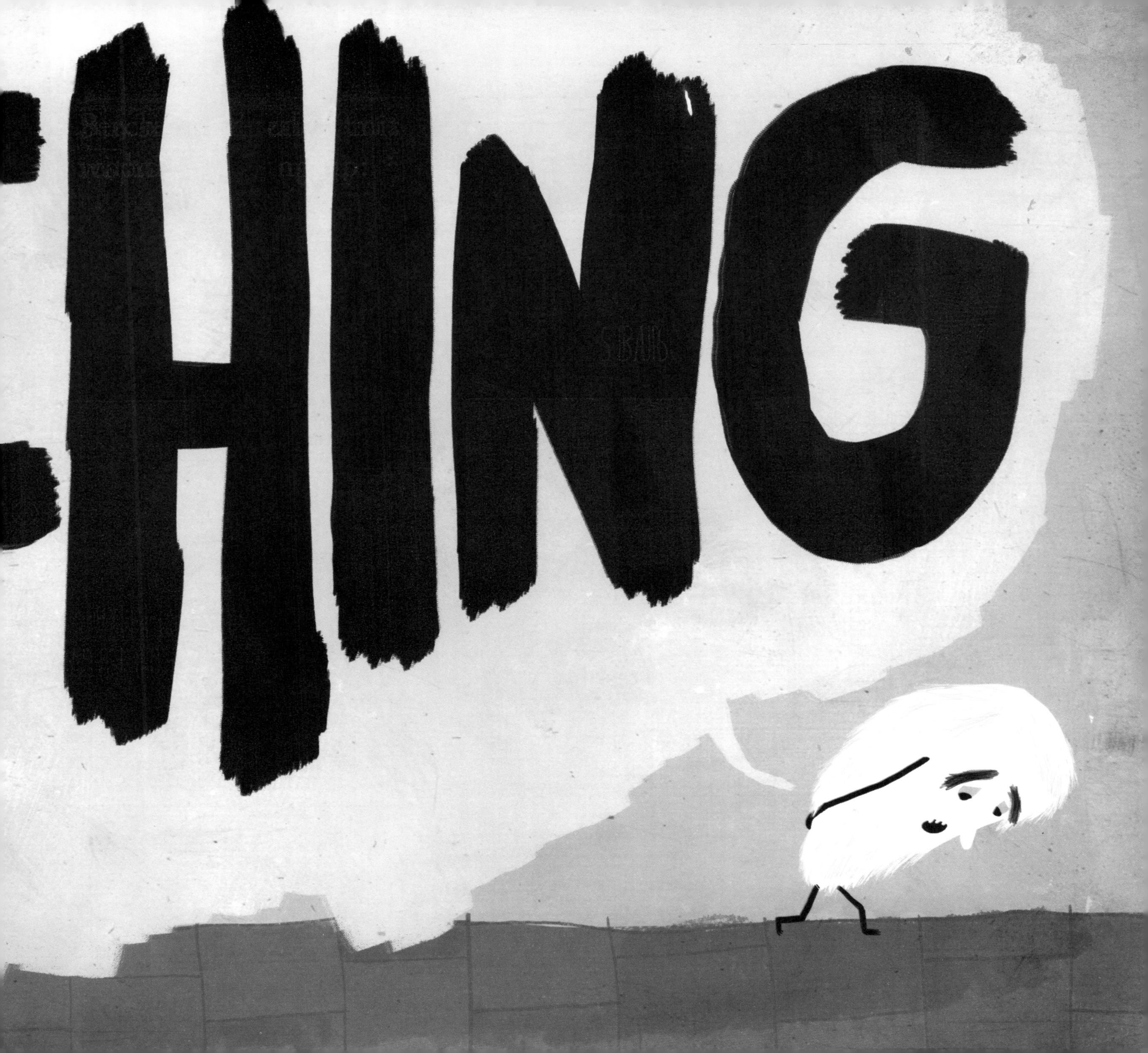
HING

Suddenly,
an unexpected thing

landed on its head.

for the first time,
it saw all of those who were around.

Serch looked a little higher and now
saw houses, one school and a cinema.
It discovered big trees and small trees,
apples, oranges and books.
It also saw   4 ANTENNAS
        23 WINDOWS
            6 BIKES
            1 PARROT

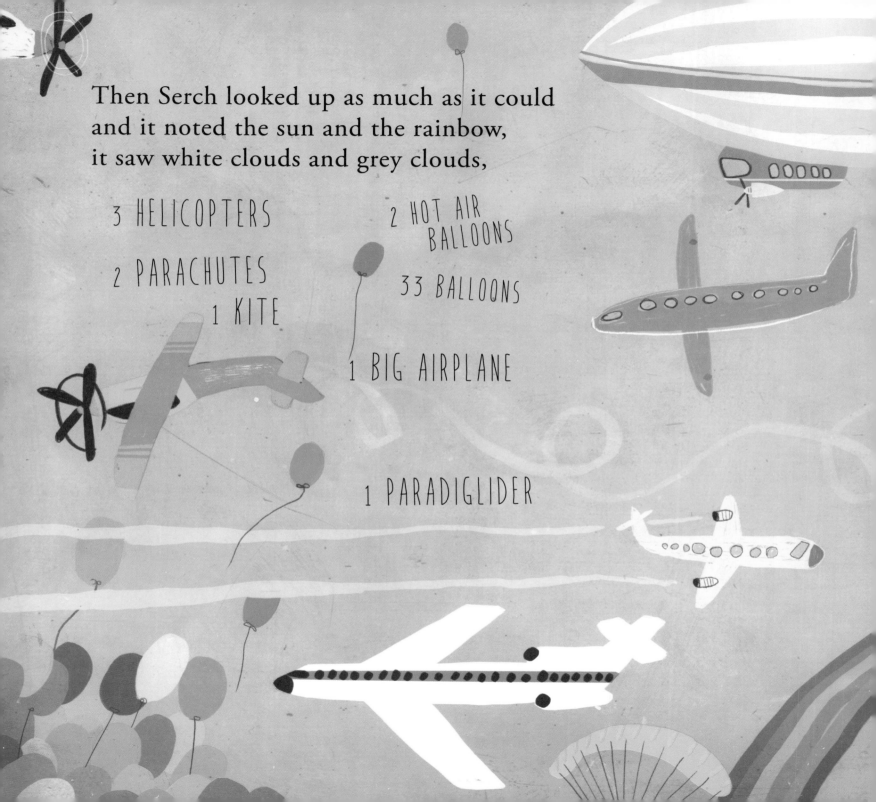

Then Serch looked up as much as it could
and it noted the sun and the rainbow,
it saw white clouds and grey clouds,

3 HELICOPTERS

2 PARACHUTES

1 KITE

2 HOT AIR
BALLOONS

33 BALLOONS

1 BIG AIRPLANE

1 PARADIGLIDER

Serch was stunned and so remained staring for a long time.

It got dark.
Serch watched the full moon
and a lot of stars.
It also saw

1 LIGHTNING
2 SATELLITES
1 SPACECRAFT
MARS, JUPITER
AND SATURN

Serch saw a shooting star
and made a wish.

From that day on
and from that night on,
Serch gave up searching
and started enjoying.

THIS STORY HAS ENDED.
HERE YOU CAN DRAW
WHATEVER YOU WANT

SERCH

BERTA

ORANGE

TEO

LOLA

LEMON

AUBERGINE

COCO

RAMONA THE BEAR

TRESH

REM

TRISH

AGILE TURTLE